12 Favorite Tales for Young Readers

MERRIGOLD PRESS • NEW YORK

Library of Conrgress Catalog Card Number:
98-83504
ISBN 0-307-37500-5

Printed in the Canada.

Note to Parents

Opening a book with your child is like opening a new world. When children are read to, they learn from an early age that books are magical. The fantastic stories, rhymes, and answers to their many questions encourage children to think, wonder, and imagine, while the quality time spent with you will help create a special bond.

The twelve stories in this collection speak directly to your child's curiosities, needs, and fears as he or she explores the world. Timeless classics and soon-to-be favorites combine in a selection that your child will want to return to again and again.

This book is also the perfect answer to your child's changing reading needs. For the pre-reader, it is a wonderful storybook, with delightful tales that appeal to the child's natural sense of wonder. As your child's vocabulary develops, he or she will delight in the short simple words and sentences that make up many of the stories. The longer, more complex constructions in other tales provide a goal for early-readers and accommodate higher levels of reading proficiency. An amazing sense of accomplishment and excitement will develop as, through the ability to read, your child's favorite stories truly become his or her own.

Childhood is a special time; never is the desire and ability to learn so acute. Developed at this age, a love of books will last a lifetime and the special time spent together sharing these stories and helping your child learn to read them will be treasured always.

The Editors of Merrigold Press,
A Division of Golden Books

First READER

12 Favorite Tales for Young Readers

The Shy Little Kitten, Page 6
by Cathleen Schurr
illustrated by Gustaf Tenggren

The Boy With a Drum, Page 29
by David L. Harrison
illustrated by Eloise Wilkin

Four Puppies, Page 53
by Anne Heathers
illustrated by Lilian Obligado

The Ugly Duckling, Page 77
by Hans Christian Andersen
illustrated by Lisa McCue

The Lively Little Rabbit, Page 101
by Ariane
illustrated by Gustaf Tenggren

A House for a Mouse, Page 125
by Kathleen N. Daly
illustrated by John P. Miller

The Little Red Hen, Page 149
a favorite folk-tale
illustrated by J.P. Miller

The Large and Growly Bear, Page 173
by Gertrude Crampton
illustrated by John P. Miller

Baby Animals, Page 197
by Garth Williams

The Cow Went Over the Mountain, Page 217
by Jeanette Krinsley
illustrated by Feodor Rojankovsky

Little Cottontail, Page 241
by Carl Memling
illustrated by Lilian Obligado

The Very Best Home For Me!, Page 265
by Jane Werner Watson
illustrated by Garth Williams

The Shy Little Kitten

pictures by
GUSTAF TENGGREN
story by
Cathleen Schurr

Way up in the hayloft of an old red barn lived a mother cat and her new baby kittens. There were five bold and frisky little roly-poly black and white kittens, and *one* little striped kitten who was very, very shy.

One day, the five bold little roly-poly black and white kittens and the one little roly-poly striped kitten who was very, very shy all sat down and washed their faces and paws with

busy little red tongues. They smoothed down their soft baby fur and stroked their whiskers and followed their mother down the ladder from the hayloft—jump, jump, jump!

Then off they marched, straight out of the cool, dark barn, into the warm sunshine. How soft the grass felt under their paws! The five bold and frisky little kittens rolled over in the grass and kicked up their heels with joy.

But the shy little striped kitten just stood off by herself at the very end of the line.

That was how she happened to see the earth push up in a little mound right in front of her. Then—*pop!*—up came a pointed little nose. The nose belonged to a chubby mole.

"Good morning!" said the mole, as friendly

as you please. "Won't you come for a walk with me?"

"Oh," said the shy little kitten. She looked shyly over her shoulder.

But the mother cat and her five bold and frisky kittens had disappeared from sight.

So the shy little kitten went walking with the chubby mole. Soon they met a speckled frog sitting near the pond.

"My, what big eyes he has!" whispered the shy little kitten. But the frog had sharp ears, too.

He chuckled. "My mouth is much bigger. Look!" And the frog opened his great cave of a mouth.

The mole and the kitten laughed and laughed until their sides ached.

When the kitten stopped laughing and looked around, the frog had vanished. On the pond, ripples spread out in great silver circles.

"I really should be getting back to my mother and the others," said the shy little kitten, "but I don't know where to find them."

"I'll show you," said a strange voice. And out of the bushes bounded a shaggy black puppy.

"Oh, thank you," said the shy kitten. "Good-bye, mole."

So off they went together, the shy kitten and the shaggy puppy dog. The little kitten, of course, kept her eyes shyly on the ground.

But the shaggy puppy stopped to bark, "Woof, woof," at a red squirrel in a tree. He was full of mischief.

"Chee, chee, chee," the squirrel chattered back. And she dropped a hickory nut right on the puppy's nose. She was very brave.

"Wow, wow, wow," barked the mischievous puppy, and off they went toward the farm.

Soon they came bounding out of the woods, and there before them stretched the farmyard.

"Here we are," said the shaggy puppy dog.

So down the hillside they raced, across the bridge above the brook, and straight on into the farmyard.

In the middle of the farmyard was the mother cat with her five bold and frisky little black and white kittens. In a flash, the mother cat was beside her shy kitten, licking her all over with a warm red tongue.

"Where have you been?" she cried. "We're all ready to start on a picnic."

The picnic was for all the farmyard animals. There were seeds for the chickens, water bugs for the ducks, and carrots and cabbages for the rabbits. There were flies for the frog, and there was a trough of mash for the pig.

Yum, yum, yum! How good it all was!

After they had finished eating, everyone was just beginning to feel comfortable and drowsy, when suddenly the frog jumped straight into the air, eyes almost popping out of his head.

"Help! Run!" he cried.

The frog made a leap for the brook.

Everyone scrambled after him and tumbled into the water.

"What is it?" asked the shy little kitten.

"A bee!" groaned the frog. "I bit a bee!"

Then they saw that one side of his mouth was puffed up like a green balloon.

Everybody laughed. They couldn't help it. Even the frog laughed. They all looked so funny as they climbed out of the brook.

The shy little kitten stood off to one side. She felt so good that she turned a backward somersault, right there in the long meadow grass. "This is the best day ever," said the shy little kitten.

There once was a boy
With a little toy drum—
Rat-a-tat-tat-a-tat
Rum-a-tum-tum.

One day he went marching
And played on his drum—
Rat-a-tat-tat-a-tat
Rum-a-tum-tum.

Soon he was joined
By a friendly old cat—
Rum-a-tum-tum-a-tum
Rat-a-tat-tat.

Next they were joined
By a green spotted frog
Who sat by the road
On an old brown log.

And then they were joined
By a big yellow dog
Who marched down the road
With the green spotted frog.

They marched by a field,
They marched by a house—
And were joined by a cow
And a furry brown mouse.

They marched by a horse
Who was pulling a plow,
And he trotted behind them
And followed the cow.

Next they were joined
By a big white duck
And an old mother chicken
With a cluck-cluck-cluck.

And a pig and a goose
And a billy goat, too,
And a big red rooster
With a cock-a-doodle-doo.

And they all went marching
With a rat-a-tat-tat,
The boy with his drum
And the big friendly cat.

The horse and the cow
And the mouse and the dog,
The duck and the chicken
And the pig and the frog.

The goose and the rooster
And the billy goat, too,
With a baaa, honk, quack,
And a cock-a-doodle-doo,

Oink, bow-wow, and a
Moo-moo-moo,
Neigh, cluck, squeak,
And a mew-mew-mew.

They all marched away
To the top of a hill—
If they haven't stopped marching,
They'll be marching still.

Four Puppies

By ANNE HEATHERS

Pictures by LILIAN OBLIGADO

There were once four new puppies who lived in a warm dark corner by the stove. Those puppies had never been outdoors because they were too little.

They didn't know about sky or trees or grass.

They didn't even know about Summer or Fall or Winter or Spring UNTIL . . .

. . . they were old enough to go out the door to the sunny porch outside.

At first the stairs were too big for the little puppies to go down. Then one day the stairs didn't look so big any more.

"They are smaller," said one puppy.

"No—we are bigger," said his brothers.

Then those four little puppies went flop, hop, and tumble, down the stairs and into the great big world outside.

They sniffed the fresh green smell of the grass.

They raced on the grass and they rolled on the grass and they turned somersaults in the grass all afternoon.

"Oh my—what a fine place this is," said the four little puppies.

Every day the four puppies went out to play.
They pounced at caterpillars.
They chased butterflies.
They ran round and round after their shadows.
They had so much fun that they hated to go inside—even when there was nice, hot chicken broth for supper!

Then one morning the stairs looked even smaller.

"And we're even bigger!" said the puppies.

And they walked down those stairs—plop! plop! plop!—as easy as pie.

But the four little puppies were so busy playing that they didn't see that the big world was changing too UNTIL . . .

. . . it had changed so much that they couldn't play the same games any more.

A funny little wind tickled their ears. They didn't have shadows because the sun was behind a cloud. The grass felt cool. The butterflies had gone. The caterpillars were hiding.

And the leaves began to turn yellow and red.

"Oh dear," said the puzzled puppies.

The next day—whoosh!—the wind knocked all the petals off a rose.

And—swoosh!—it blew the leaves right off the trees.

Those four puppies tried to put the petals back on the rose.

They tried to put the leaves back on the trees.

But they couldn't, so they started to cry.

"You silly-billies—there's nothing to cry about," said a friendly red squirrel in the hickory tree.

"When the leaves turn red and yellow and come off the trees it means that SUMMER is over and FALL has come. Why, you'll just have more fun than ever!"

And the squirrel was right.

Leaves as crisp as cornflakes covered the ground.

The four little puppies scuffed around in leaves and buried themselves under leaves and kicked leaves up in the air.

They had so much fun that they hated to go inside — even when there were lamb chops for supper!

Then one morning when the puppies went out to play they didn't have to walk — plop! plop! — down the stairs. They could jump down the steps two at a time.

"They are even smaller," said one puppy.

"No—we are even bigger," said his brothers.

But they didn't see that the big world was changing too UNTIL . . .

. . . it had changed so much that they couldn't play the same games any more. The water in the puddles was as hard as glass. A rough wind blew their ears back, and blew the leaves clear out of the yard.

"Oh dear," cried the puzzled little puppies.

They tried to hold onto the leaves, but still they blew away, faster and faster.

So the puppies started to cry.

"You silly-billies—there's nothing to cry about," said the friendly red squirrel in the hickory tree. "When there's ice on the puddles and the North Wind blows it means that Fall is over and Winter has come. You'll just have more fun than ever!"

And the squirrel was right—for the next day when the puppies went out to play, everything was white with snow!

Every day after that those four little puppies parted snow with their noses and slid down the bank and made footprints in the snow.

They had so much fun that they hated to go inside—even when there were great big beef bones for supper!

One morning the puppies were so big they could jump down the stairs three at a time.

But they didn't notice that the big world was changing too UNTIL...

...it had changed so much that they couldn't play the same games any more.

The sunshine was warmer. It wasn't raining, but the water kept drip-dripping from the trees. The snow bank was too small to slide down.

And the next day there were bare brown patches of ground with no snow at all!

"Oh dear," cried the puzzled little puppies. They tried to push the snow into a pile so they could keep it to play with. But the snow turned to water and sank into the ground right under their paws. So the puppies started to cry.

"You silly-billies—there's nothing to cry about," said the friendly red squirrel in the hickory tree.

"When the sun gets warmer and melts the snow it means that WINTER is over and SPRING has come—and you'll soon guess for yourselves what comes after Spring. It's like a wheel turning round and round."

And the squirrel was right.

Some tiny green stalks poked up out of the ground. The puppies and the stalks grew bigger every day. And one day the puppies jumped down all the steps at once and found leaves and flowers on every stalk.

"That's how the big world looked when we first saw it!" they cried.

And they began to bark happily, for they had guessed what comes after Spring.

"SUMMER is what comes after Spring!" cried the first puppy. "Butterflies again!"

"Then Fall," said the second puppy. "Crisp leaves again!"

"Then Winter," said the third puppy. "Nice white snow again!"

"Then Spring," said the fourth puppy. "Brand-new leaves again!"

"AND EVERYTHING STARTS ALL OVER AGAIN EVERY SPRING!" all the puppies cried together.

The friendly red squirrel looked down at them from the hickory tree.

"Now that you know all that, you are not puzzled little puppies any more," he said.

"What are we then?" asked the puppies.

"You are big brave dogs," he said.

And the squirrel was right— as usual.

The UGLY DUCKLING

By Hans Christian Andersen
Illustrated by Lisa McCue

One summer day a mother duck's eggs began to crack. Six little ducklings broke out from their shells. "Peep, peep," they cried.

"Are you all here?" the mother asked. "One, two, three, four, five, six," she counted. One egg, much bigger than all the others, had not yet hatched. So the mother duck sat and sat on that big egg, and at last it began to crack. "Peep, peep," cried the new duckling.

Leading her brood to the pond, the mother gasped when she saw the new duckling waddling along, for he was big and ugly. "He does not look like the others," she thought. "I wonder if he can swim."

The ducklings splashed into the water, with the strange ugly duckling last of all. He swam merrily with the rest.

The mother was pleased. After a long swim, she marched her children into the barnyard to meet the other birds.

"Look at that big ugly one!" some ducks murmured. They began to laugh and peck at him.

"Leave him alone!" cried the mother. "He swims well, and he will grow to be a fine drake, I'm sure!"

But day after day the poor duckling's life in the barnyard grew worse. Not only did the ducks make fun of him, but the chickens and turkeys did as well. Finally he could stand no more teasing and ran away.

The duckling soon came to a swamp that was surrounded by woods. He fell asleep among the rushes, under a friendly moon.

The duckling stayed alone in the rushes for two whole days. Then two wild geese came by, wanting to pass the time.

"You are so ugly that I like you," one of them said. "Come with us, and we will introduce you to some other geese."

But before they could go, a great *bang, bang* rang through the woods. In a flash, the two wild geese were gone.

Hunters and their dogs were coming through the woods.

The duckling looked about him. In the distance he saw an enormous dog, with its tongue hanging out of its mouth.

The dog came closer and closer. But after a good look at the ugly duckling, it barked and ran off another way.

"Thank goodness!" the ugly duckling cried.

When he was sure it was quite safe, the ugly duckling spread his wings and began to fly away. Flying was difficult, for it was his first flight and there was a strong wind. But he kept on till evening, when he came to a little tumbledown cottage.

The tired bird slipped inside the cottage. It belonged to an old woman who lived there with a tomcat and a hen.

"What good luck!" said the old woman when she saw the ugly duckling. "We shall have duck's eggs to eat, if this duck doesn't turn out to be a drake."

The hen and the tomcat crept quite close to the drake.
"Can you lay eggs?" the hen asked.
"Can you purr or arch your back?" the tomcat asked.
"No," said the young drake. "But I can swim and fly."

“Swim? Fly?” the hen cackled. “What earthly good is swimming or flying? You should learn to lay eggs.”

“Or purr,” added the grinning tomcat.

“I had best be on my way,” said the drake, whose heart was beating quite fast. He left the cottage at once and flew to a marsh.

Outside, the autumn winds were howling. The young drake was happy to swim and dive in the water, but he felt all alone.

One frosty evening a flock of beautiful white birds flew overhead. The young drake felt strange when he saw them. He cried out to them and spun around in the water. But soon the large birds were out of sight.

The weather grew colder, and one night the pond froze. The drake was stuck fast in the ice.

The next morning a kind peasant came by. When he saw the shivering bird, he broke the ice with his wooden clogs and carried him home.

The peasant's children wanted to play with the bird, and they began to chase him. He flew up in panic, knocking over a pitcher of milk. It crashed to the floor along with some china.

"Oh!" the peasant's wife cried, raising her hands in anger. This frightened the bird still more. He flew into the new butter, and then into the flour bin.

"Out of my house, before you spoil all the food!" the woman cried, and she drove the young drake outdoors again.

For the rest of the winter the drake slept in the marsh grass.

When the sun began to shine warm again, he awoke. His feathers were a lighter color now. And when he stretched his wings, he found that they were big and strong. How good it felt to fly under the warm sunshine!

The drake flew until he came to a splendid garden. There was a pond, and on it glided three of the beautiful white birds he had seen before.

The drake fluttered down onto the water. "They will not let me swim with them," he thought sadly, "but at least I can gaze at them in all their beauty."

The swans swam closer, and the drake bowed his head as they passed. But there, as he looked into the water, what did he see . . .

A graceful, long-necked white bird looked back at him, and this bird was lovelier than all the others.

The drake had been a swan all along, though none had known it. And now all the beautiful swans were gathering about to welcome him.

Two children ran into the garden. “Look, look!” cried the boy. “There is a new swan!”

“He is the loveliest of all,” said the girl.

The swan was filled with joy. “I never thought I should know such happiness,” he said to himself, “when I was but an ugly duckling.”

THE Lively Little Rabbit

By ARIANE

Illustrated by GUSTAF TENGGREN

Way back in the woods lived a lively little rabbit. All day long he nibbled leaves and roots and played with his brothers and sisters. Most of the day they would slide down a big hill, and the lively little rabbit was always in front, the first one to reach the bottom.

All the little rabbits would have had a wonderful time—except for the weasel who lived in a hole in the forest. That old weasel was mean and grumpy and always pushing his sharp nose into everything. Besides, he was always ready to eat little rabbits for breakfast.

So the lively little rabbit, who didn't want

to be eaten for breakfast, was very careful to keep out of the weasel's way. So were his brothers and sisters. Whenever they saw the mean old weasel coming, they jumped quickly into their hole and stayed there until it was safe to come out again. And the lively little rabbit was always the first one down the hole.

The weasel was a very cunning weasel, too. One day, when the lively little rabbit was alone in his hole, the weasel wriggled down into it by the back door. For a minute, the lively little

rabbit thought he was going to be eaten for breakfast. But he was smart, and quick as a flash he jumped out of the front door and began to run as fast as he could.

He ran and ran until he came to the end of the forest. There were big hills, and roads going up and down, and a little village.

But the lively little rabbit only wanted his dinner.

"Oh, my!" he said. "I am so hungry I could eat two hundred thousand million big carrots right now!"

A red squirrel, who lived with his family in a near-by tree, heard this remark. In one glide and two jumps and three hops he reached a garden and came back with a bunch of delicious carrots.

"Oh, thank you, red squirrel!" said the lively little rabbit, very pleased. "I love carrots. You are a friend indeed."

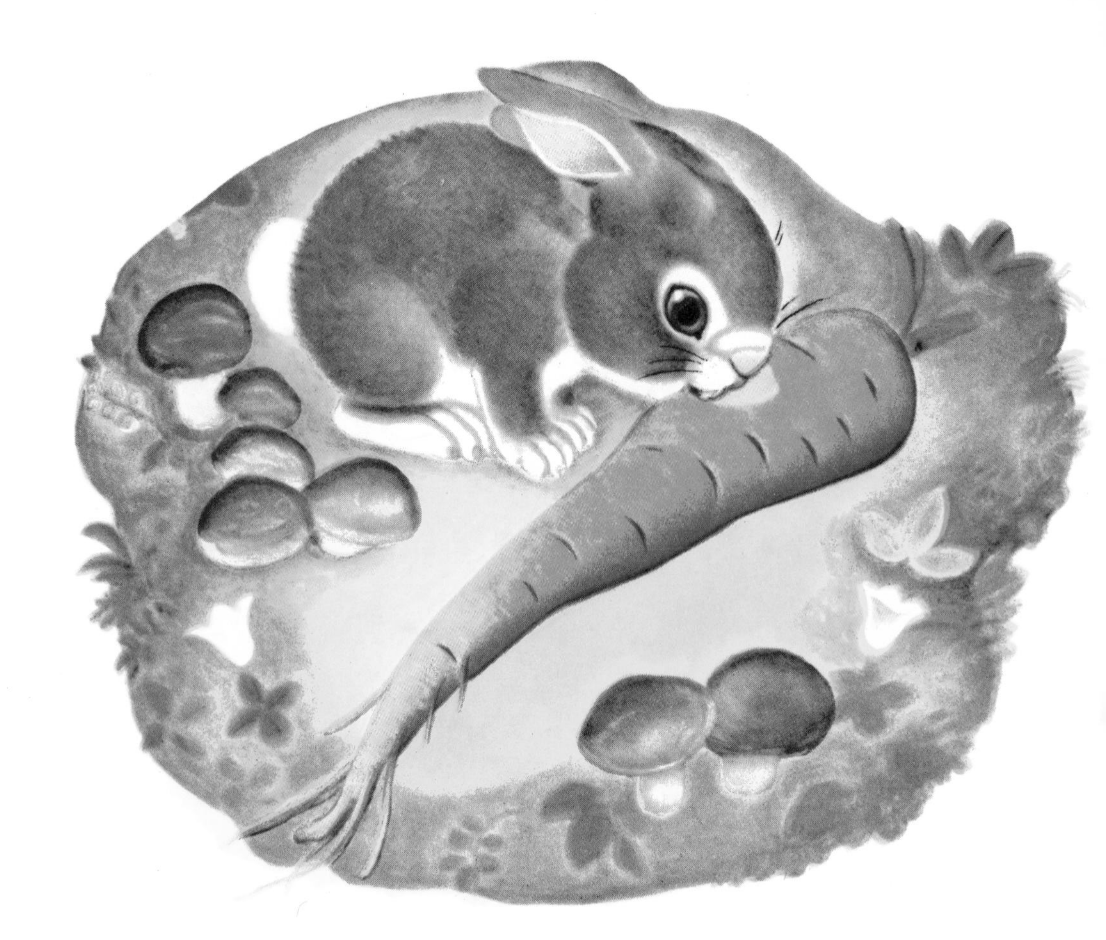

After the rabbit had eaten all his carrots, he decided to spend the night with his new friend.

At first he thought it was a funny idea to sleep way up in a tree. But the red squirrel pushed and shoved him until they were both settled, snug and peaceful, high up in the tree under the stars.

The next day the lively little rabbit tried and tried to remember his way home, but he could not, so the red squirrel brought him to the wise old owl. As soon as it was dark the owl spread his wings in search of the rabbit's home.

In no time at all the owl had found it and he swooped down to tell the news to all the brothers and sisters.

The little rabbits didn't have to wait long.

"Here they come! Here they come!" they all cried at once.

And sure enough, there came the owl, flying

close to the ground to show the way to the lively little rabbit, who was hopping along just as fast as he could go. The red squirrel was hopping along, too. He had come for a visit.

"Hello! What's the news?" said the lively little rabbit.

"Oh, dear!" cried the little rabbits. "The mean old weasel came again this morning and ate our great grandmother on Daddy's side for breakfast!"

This made the lively little rabbit very sad.

"Something must be done," he said.

"What?" said the other little rabbits.

"I think I know," said the wise squirrel. "We must give that weasel a terrible, terrible scare."

And he told all the little rabbits his plan. It was a wonderful idea. They were going to build a make-believe dragon out of leaves and twigs.

They would all crawl inside to make it go, and the lively little rabbit was to pretend to be the head.

Early next morning they set to work, and the wise squirrel fixed the lively little rabbit up to make him look very fierce indeed.

Soon the dragon was ready. The squirrel and the rabbits looked at their work with pride. It was so very funny, especially when the

owl, who was hidden inside with the rabbits, flapped his wings and shouted: "Ooo! Ooo!"

What a wonderful dragon it was!

Meanwhile the mean old weasel was waking up for the day. He stretched and he yawned and he growled and he said to himself:

"Humm. Now what about breakfast . . . ?"

But just as the mean old weasel came to the top of the hill, up popped the make-believe dragon. It flapped its wings and wiggled its tail and shouted in a very loud voice: "Ooo! Ooo! Ooo!"

The weasel was terribly frightened. He was so scared that for a minute he couldn't move at all. Then he turned around and ran.

He ran away so fast that he would still be running if he had not stumbled on a rock. But he did, and he rolled to the bottom of the hill. There he picked himself up and began to run away again.

All day long, way back in the woods, the lively little rabbit danced with his brothers and sisters and their friend the wise red squirrel. Everyone was very happy.

The sleepy owl asked to be excused and went to bed.

The very next day the mean old weasel, who was still full of bumps and bruises, moved far away from the woods. Never again has he ever tried to eat a lively little rabbit for breakfast.

A House for a Mouse

Written by Kathleen N. Daly
Illustrated by John P. Miller

Jonathan Mouse woke up with raindrops splashing on his head.

"It's time to find a real house to live in," he said. "Time to settle down!"

So into the street went Jonathan, whistling a cheerful tune and merrily jumping in and out of puddles.

Soon Jonathan was in the country.

The sun was shining, the flowers were blooming, a butterfly was flitting, and Duck was swimming in the pond with her new ducklings.

"Hello, Duck," said Jonathan. "Where do you live?"

"Here in the reeds," said Duck. "Come and see."

Duck and her ducklings paddled off. Jonathan Mouse jumped in after them.

"Oh, no!" said Jonathan. "This water is cold and wet!"

"Come and see my home," called Frog, diving under a lily pad.

"No, thanks," said Jonathan Mouse with a shiver. "Homes for ducks and frogs are TOO WET for a mouse!"

Jonathan Mouse was drying off in the sun when along came Bird.

"Come and see my home," said Bird.

Bird flew into a tree, and Jonathan scampered up after her.

"Oh, dear," said Jonathan. "It's a lovely nest for a bird—but birds can fly, and I can't! Thanks anyway!"

On his way down the tree Jonathan saw Squirrel peering out of his hole.

"Come on in," said Squirrel.

"No, thanks," said Jonathan. "Homes for birds and squirrels are much TOO HIGH UP for a mouse!"

Thump thump thump came the footsteps of a friendly brown bear.

"Come and see where I live," said Bear.

But when they got to Bear's cave, Jonathan Mouse felt a little scared.

"It's a lovely home for a bear," he said. "But it's much TOO BIG for a mouse. Thanks anyway!"

Hippity-hop, along came Rabbit.

"My house is much better," she said. "Come with me!"

When they got to Rabbit's hole, three baby rabbits squeaked and squealed and jumped all over Jonathan Mouse.

"Oh, dear," he said. "You are very nice rabbits in a very nice home—but you are much TOO NOISY for a mouse like me!"

As Jonathan Mouse sat panting outside the rabbit hole, who should come along but Fox.

Fox smiled a big, toothy smile at Jonathan.

"Come home with me," he said. "I'll show you a really nice home."

Jonathan Mouse followed Fox.

Soon they came to a hole, and Fox smiled some more.

"Do come in, dear Mouse," he said.

But Jonathan Mouse ran off, saying, "Thanks anyway, Fox—your TEETH are TOO BIG for me!"

Jonathan Mouse ran and ran until suddenly he bumped into another mouse and they both fell over.

"How nice to meet you, Jonathan Mouse," said the other mouse. "I hear you are looking for a house. So am I. My name is Emily Mouse. There's a farm here where everybody has a house. Let's go see!"

So off they went to visit the farm, Jonathan Mouse and Emily Mouse.

Yes, everyone on the farm had a home.

Dog lived in the doghouse.

Hen and Rooster and Chick lived in the chicken coop.

Horse lived in the stable.

Cow lived in the barn.

"But, there doesn't seem to be a house for a mouse," said Emily with a sigh.

"No," said Jonathan with another sigh.

From his perch up above, Blue Jay heard those sad little sighs.

"Come, follow me," he said. "I know the very place for you two."

"There!" said Blue Jay.

"Oh, what a pretty house!" said Emily. "It looks like a doll's house!"

"It just needs a little straightening up," said Jonathan.

Emily and Jonathan pushed and pulled and heaved and grunted, and pretty soon that little house was as straight up as any house ever was.

"Oh, thank you, Blue Jay," said Emily and Jonathan.

Jonathan found a toolbox, with tools just the right size for a mouse—or two.

Emily found some clothes, just the right size for a mouse—or two.

Then the two little mice swept and dusted and painted and tidied.

Jonathan sawed wood.
Emily planted a garden.

And when it grew dark, they put on their aprons and cooked a fine stew—those two.

Then Emily Mouse and Jonathan Mouse sat down to supper in a house that was just exactly right for a mouse—or two.

The Little RED HEN

A FAVORITE FOLK-TALE

Pictures by J. P. MILLER

One summer day the little Red Hen found a grain of wheat.

"A grain of wheat!" said the little Red Hen to herself. "I will plant it."

She asked the duck:
"Will you help me plant this grain of wheat?"
"Not I!" said the duck.

She asked the goose:
"Will you help me plant this grain of wheat?"
"Not I!" said the goose.

She asked the cat:
"Will you help me plant this grain of wheat?"
"Not I!" said the cat.

She asked the pig:
"Will you help me plant this grain of wheat?"
"Not I!" said the pig.

"Then I will plant it myself," said the little Red Hen. And she did.

Soon the wheat grew tall, and the little Red Hen knew it was time to reap it.

"Who will help me reap the wheat?" she asked.

"Not I!" said the duck.

"Not I!" said the goose.

"Not I!" said the cat.

"Not I!" said the pig.

"Then I will reap it myself,"
said the little Red Hen.
And she did.

She reaped the wheat, and it was ready to be taken to the mill and made into flour.

"Who will help me carry the wheat to the mill?" she asked.

"Not I!" said the duck.
"Not I!" said the goose.
"Not I!" said the cat.
"Not I!" said the pig.

"Then I will carry it myself," said the little Red Hen. And she did. She carried the wheat to the mill, and the miller made it into flour.

When she got home, she asked, "Who will help me make the flour into dough?"

"Not I!" said the duck.

"Not I!" said the goose.

"Not I!" said the cat.

"Not I!" said the pig.

"Then I will make the dough myself," said the little Red Hen. And she did.

Soon the bread was ready to go into the oven.

"Who will help me bake the bread?" said the little Red Hen.

"Not I!" said the duck.

"Not I!" said the goose.

"Not I!" said the cat.

"Not I!" said the pig.

"Then I will bake it myself," said the little Red Hen. And she did.

After the loaf had been taken from the oven it was set on the window sill to cool.

"And now," said the little Red Hen, "who will help me to eat the bread?"

"I will!" said the duck.

"I will!" said the goose.

"I will!" said the cat.

"I will!" said the pig.

"No, I will eat it myself!" said the little Red Hen. And she did.

THE EGG AND I

THE LARGE AND GROWLY BEAR

BY GERTRUDE CRAMPTON

ILLUSTRATED BY JOHN P. MILLER

For Maureen

Once there was a large and growly bear. One spring morning, he woke up with nothing to do.

"I know!" said the large and growly bear. "I will find someone to frighten! That is just what a large and growly bear needs."

So the large
and growly bear
went growling
and prowling
and scowling,

looking for
someone to frighten.
And what did he see?

He saw the bluebirds.
The bluebirds were busy,
for it was spring.
They were flying here

and pulling up a worm there

and hurrying home to their babies.

“I can frighten bluebirds,”
said the large and growly bear.
So he took a deep breath,
and it came out, “GRRRR!”

“Ssssh!” said the bluebirds.
“You will wake up the babies!”

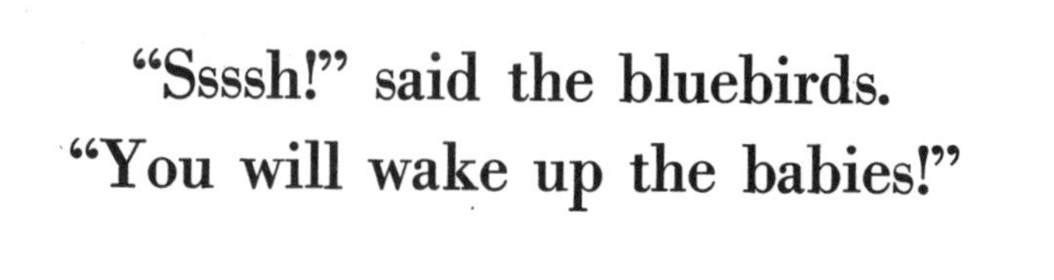

“But I mean it,” said the large
and growly bear.
“I am frightening you!”

"Not now," said the bluebirds. "We are too busy flying here and pulling up a worm there

and hurrying home to our babies. Find someone else to frighten."

"Well, I never!" said the large
and growly bear to himself.
"There must be someone I can frighten!"
So the large and growly bear
went growling and prowling and scowling,
looking for someone to frighten.

And what did he see?

He saw the rabbits.
The rabbits were happy, for it was spring.
They were jumping here

and hopping there

and bouncing
like balls with pink ears.

"I can frighten rabbits," said the large and growly bear.

So he took a big, deep breath, and it came out, "GRRRRRR!"

"Ssssh!" said the rabbits. "You will mix us up. We are counting our bounces."

"But I mean it," said the large and growly bear. "I am frightening you!"

"Not now," said the rabbits. "We are too busy jumping here and hopping there and bouncing like balls with pink ears. Find someone else to frighten."

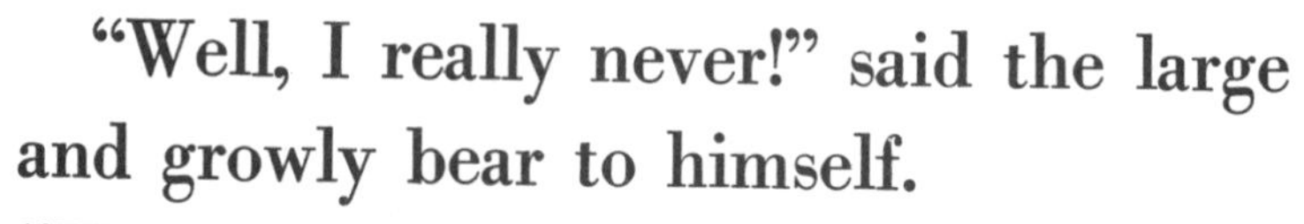

"Well, I really never!" said the large
and growly bear to himself.
"There must be someone I can frighten!"

So the large and growly bear
went growling and prowling and scowling,
looking for someone to frighten.

And what did he see?

He saw the moles.
They were little and
as soft as silk, for it
was spring.

They were digging dirt here
and moving dirt there

and making tunnels
halfway to China.

"I can frighten moles," said the large and growly bear.

So he took a great big, deep breath, and it came out, "GRRRRRRRR!"

"Ssssh!" said the moles.
"You will shake the tunnels to China!"
"But I mean it," said the large
and growly bear. "I am frightening you!"

"Not now," said the moles.
"We are too busy digging dirt
here and moving dirt there
and making tunnels halfway to China.
Find someone else to frighten."

"Well, I really,
really never!"
said the large
and growly bear.

"A large and growly bear
must have someone to frighten.
He just must!"

The large and growly bear
was tired and cross and very growly,
but all at once he had an idea.

“Fish are never too busy to be frightened,”
said the large and growly bear.
“I will go to the shining, silver river.
I will find some little fish,
and I will frighten them half to death.”

The large and growly bear
walked softly, softly.
No one could hear.
The large and growly bear
walked slowly, slowly.
He held all his breath
for an *enormous*
GRRRRRRRR!

At last the large and growly bear came to the shining, silver river. The large and growly bear still held his breath for an *enormous*

GRRRRRRRR!

Then the large and growly bear looked into the shining, silver river. He did not see any little fish.

He saw

A VERY LARGE
AND
GROWLY BEAR.

"Oh, my paws and claws!" cried the large and growly bear.

Suddenly he felt very small. He didn't feel growly, but he did feel like hurrying.

"Hurry!" he cried. "Hurry away from the large and growly bear!"

So he hurried. "Fly!" he shouted to the bluebirds. "Hop!" he shouted to the rabbits.

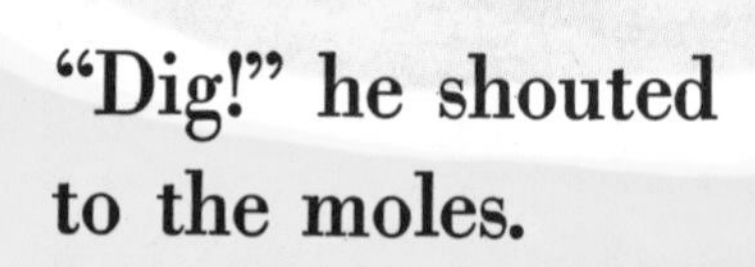

"Dig!" he shouted to the moles.

The bluebirds and the rabbits
and the moles laughed.
They knew the shining, silver river
and the tricks it played.

"Did you find someone to frighten?"
they called.

"Yes!" said the large and growly bear.

"Who?" called the bluebirds
and the rabbits and the moles.
The large and growly bear
poked his nose out of his door.
He cried, in a small
and not growly voice,

"ME!"

Baby Animals

· BY GARTH WILLIAMS

Baby Fox is full of mischief. He is hoping he will find a sleepy rabbit to chase, but the rabbits are hiding.

Baby Sheep is dancing over the hills and meadows. It is spring, and everyone wants to dance in the warm sunshine.

Baby Opossum is pretending to be dead. If a big dog comes along, she will play dead. Then the dog will go away.

Baby Skunk is fooled by her play-
mate's lying so still.

Baby Lion roars, "Ahrrroum!" and sounds almost like his father. One day he hopes he will be king of the jungle.

Baby Tiger says, "You frighten me!" Baby Tiger looks like a great big kitten, and he loves to play like one.

Baby Giraffe is so tall that she has to bend down to stay in the picture. She never makes a sound, and she can run very fast.

Baby Monkey swings from branch to branch. He holds on with his hands, with his feet, and with his tail.

Baby Orangutan also lives in the trees. She puts a leaf on her head to keep the sun off.

Baby Kangaroo practices taking long hops. He uses his big tail for balance so he won't fall.

Baby Koala lives in Australia, like Baby Kangaroo. She sleeps in the branches of the eucalyptus tree and eats its leaves.

Baby Woodchuck has been asleep all winter long. Now she is eating tender grass and a small, tasty root. Soon she will be very plump.

Baby Mink has just caught her first fish. She will show it to her mother and then eat it for breakfast.

Baby Rabbit has hopped away from his mother's side. His eyes are wide-open. He sees a big bumblebee. "I don't think I will go any farther," he says.

Baby Raccoon washes her apple. She never eats anything until she has washed it first. She even washes a fish.

Baby Camel walks very well and can go for a day without drinking. He keeps food and water in his fat humps.

Baby Owl says, "Whooooooo's undressed, and whooooooo's in bed, and whooooooo's asleep?"

The Cow Went Over The Mountain

By Jeanette Krinsley
Illustrated by Feodor Rojankovsky

One day Little Cow said to her mother,
"I'm going over to the other mountain.
The grass is munchier over there."
"Very well," said Mother Cow.

So away went Little Cow,
and soon she met a little frog.

"Come along with me, Little Frog," she said.
"I'm going over to the other mountain.
The bugs are much crunchier there."

So Little Frog jumped up on Cow's back,
and they walked along together.
Soon they met a little white duck.

"Come with us,"
said Cow to Little White Duck.
"We are going to the other mountain.
The water is much sploshier there."
So Duck went too.

Down the road they walked
till they met a pig.
"Come along with us, Little Pig," said Cow.
"We are going over to the other mountain.
The mud is much sloshier there."

So Pig went too,
and they walked along together
and sang a silly song.

"The grass is munchier.
The bugs are crunchier."

"The water is sploshier.
The mud is sloshier."
Then they saw a bear, so they sang,
"The honey is gooier."

And Bear said, "I'll come too."
And they walked and walked and walked.

When they got to the other mountain,
they all sat down to rest.

And they were so tired
that they soon fell asleep.

In the morning they woke with the sun,
very hungry and all ready to eat.
BUT—

The grass was not munchier.

The bugs were not crunchier.

The water was not splashier.

The mud was not sloshier.

The honey was not gooier.
It just was not true,
all that Little Cow had said.
And everyone felt sad and blue,
till all at once Cow jumped up.

"Look," she said.
"We are on the wrong mountain."
And as she pointed they all agreed
that the other mountain was greener.

So they started out again
and walked and walked and walked.

Down, down, down they went
till they came to the bottom of the mountain.
Then—

Up, up, up they climbed.
Then they stopped,
and what do you think they found?

They were home, on their own green mountain.
So they all looked at Cow and sang—

"The grass is munchier.
The bugs are crunchier.
The water is sploshier.
The mud is sloshier.
The honey is gooier,
Right here at home."

And they laughed and laughed and laughed.

Little Cottontail

BY CARL MEMLING

PICTURES BY LILIAN OBLIGADO

Once there was a little cottontail rabbit who lived in a cozy nest.

"Mother," said the little cottontail, "when will I grow up?"

"Soon," said his mother.

"But first, Little Cottontail, you must leave the nest."

"Leave the nest?" he said.

His little round nest was just the right size. It was soft and warm with a bed made of grass and tufts of fur. It was a nice nest.

A mother and a father robin peered down at him. Their babies were still too young to leave the nest. They wondered what Little Cottontail would do.

With a flop and a hop, and a hump and a bump, Little Cottontail left the nest.

"NOW am I grown up?" he asked.

His mother smiled. "Not yet," she said. "First, Little Cottontail, you must learn to wash yourself."

"Please teach me," he said.

"Watch closely," said the mother.

A porcupine sitting on a hollow log watched closely, too.

"This is the way you wash yourself early in the morning.

"Shake your feet, one at a time. Then lick them clean, one at a time.

"Scrub your face with your little front paws.

"Scratch your ears with your big hind paws.

"Then fluff all your fur up, and lick it clean—and you'll be bright and shining early in the morning."

"I can do all that," said Little Cottontail.

And he did.

"Didn't he do that very well!" a deermouse whispered to her tiny children.

"NOW am I grown up?" asked Little Cottontail.

"Not yet," said his mother.

"First, Little Cottontail, you must learn what big rabbits eat...

"Out in the meadow all summer long, they eat grass and herbs and lots of green plants.

"Over by the farmhouse all summer long, they eat carrots and cabbage and nice fresh fruit.

"All through the winter, white with snow, they eat buds and twigs and the bark of trees.

"These are things that big rabbits eat whenever they are hungry."

Little Cottontail said, "I listened closely, and I think I know them."

And he did.

"NOW am I grown up?" asked Little Cottontail.

"Not yet!" hissed a woodchuck, popping up from his burrow. "First you must learn about foxes!"

"What about foxes?" said Little Cottontail.

"Foxes like to chase rabbits," said his mother. "They like to catch them for dinner.

"You must learn how to tell that a fox is coming. Please, Little Cottontail, watch very closely . . .

"This is the way you twitch your nose—*sniff-sniff, sniff-sniff . . . sniff-sniff-sniff*—to sniff the air for the smell of a fox.

"And this is the way you cock your ears, and raise your head, and glance about—to see if that bad fox is coming near.

"And if the fox comes, this is the way you lay back your ears and bound away. This is the way you hop, hop, hop as fast as you can, before the fox can catch you.

"You dodge and you twist and you take short cuts.

"You zigzag and circle and double back on your tracks.

"You lead the fox to a brier patch. You do a quick-quick stop there, and hop to the side. You freeze like a statue—and the fox runs by.

"And all that the fox ever does catch, is a pawful of thorns in the brier patch."

"That's so much to learn," said Little Cottontail. "Though I did listen closely.

"Now let me see. What came first? . . . Oh, yes. First I must twitch my nose."

So Little Cottontail twitched his nose to sniff the air for the smell of a fox. Then he cocked his ears and he glanced about . . .

"Mother!" cried Little Cottontail. "A FOX *IS* COMING!"

Into the hollow log sprang the porcupine. The deermouse scampered off swiftly with her tiny children. Down popped the woodchuck into his burrow. And "Chee chee!" cried the robin as he flew away.

Little Cottontail and his mother laid back their ears and bounded away—and the fox chased after them! "Oh, dear," thought the mother. "What if Little Cottontail doesn't remember all I told him?"

But Little Cottontail zigzagged

and circled

and

doubled back on his tracks.

And then he came to a quick-quick stop and hopped to the side.

He froze like a statue—and the fox ran by, straight into the thorns of a brier patch!

"Mother," said the cottontail, gasping for breath. "NOW am I grown up?"

"Yes," said his mother. "Now you are grown up—BIG COTTONTAIL!"

The Very Best Home for Me!

Originally published as *Animal Friends*

By Jane Werner Watson

Pictures by
Garth Williams

OUR HOUSE

ONCE upon a time, in a small house deep in the woods, lived a lively family of animals.

There were Miss Kitty and Mr. Pup, Brown Bunny, Little Chick, Fluffy Squirrel, Poky Turtle, and Tweeter Bird.

Each had his little chest and his little bed and chair, and they took turns cooking on their little kitchen stove.

They got along nicely when it came to sharing toys, being quiet at nap times and keeping the house neat. But they could not agree on food.

When Miss Kitty cooked, they had milk and catnip tea and little bits of liver on their plates.

Pup didn't mind the liver, but the rest were unhappy.

They didn't like any better the bones Pup served them in his turn. Nor Bunny's carrot dinners, or Tweeter's tasty worms, or Turtle's ants' eggs, or Squirrel's nuts.

When Bunny fixed the meals, she arranged lettuce leaves and carrot nibbles with artistic taste, but only Tweeter Bird would eat any of them. And when Tweeter served worms and crisp chewy seeds only Little Chick would eat them.

And Little Chick liked bugs and beetles even better. Poky Turtle would nibble at them, but what he really hungered for were tasty ants' eggs.

Fluffy Squirrel wanted nuts and nuts and nuts. Without his sharp teeth and his firm paws, the others could not get a nibble from a nut, so they all went hungry when Fluffy got the meals.

Finally they all knew something must be done. They gathered around the fire one cool and cozy evening and talked things over.

"The home for me," said Mr. Pup, "is a place where I can have bones and meat every day."

"I want milk and liver instead of bugs and seeds," said Miss Kitty.

"Nuts for me," said Squirrel.

"Ants' eggs," yawned Turtle.

"Crispy lettuce," whispered Bunny.

"A stalk of seeds," dreamed Bird, "and some worms make a home for me."

"New homes are what we need," said Mr. Pup. And everyone agreed. So next morning they packed their little satchels and they said their fond good-by's.

Squirrel waved good-by to them all. For he had decided to stay in the house in the woods.

He started right in to gather nuts.

Soon there were nuts in the kitchen stove, nuts in the cupboards, nuts piled up in all the empty beds. There was scarcely room for that happy little Squirrel.

The others hopped along till they came to a garden with rows and rows of tasty growing things. "Here's the home for me," said bright-eyed Brown Bunny, and she settled down there at the roots of a big tree.

Little Chick found a chicken yard full of lovely scratchy gravel where lived all kinds of crispy, crunchy bugs.

"Here I stay," chirped Chick, squeezing under the fence to join the other chickens there.

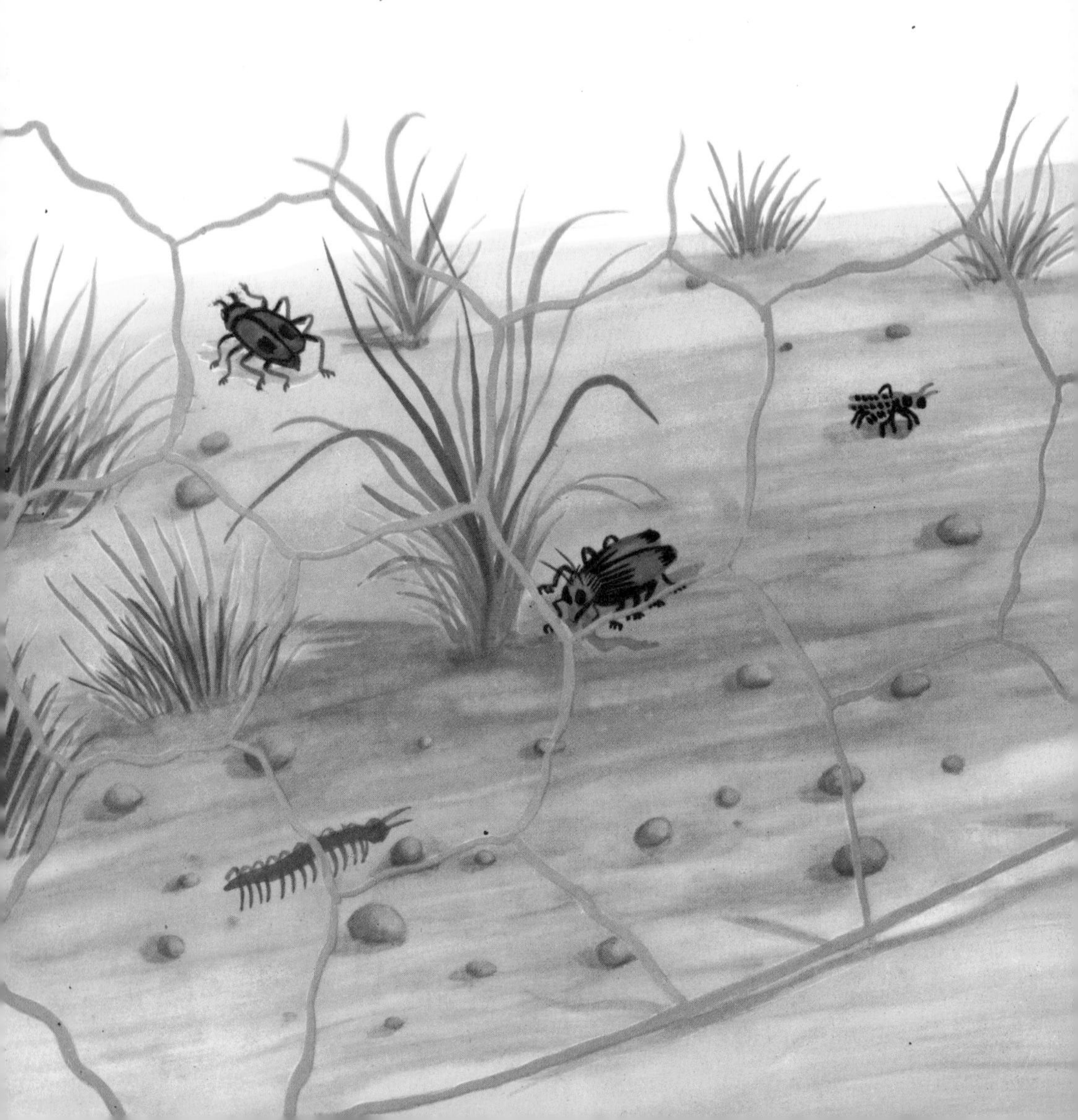

Poky Turtle found a pond with a lovely log for napping, half in the sun, half in the shade.

Close by the log was a busy, bustling ant hill, full of the eggs Turtle loved.

Tweeter Bird found a nest in a tree above the pond, where he could see the world, the seeds on the grasses, and the worms on the ground.

"This is the home for me," sang Bird happily.

Miss Kitty went on till she came to a house where a little girl welcomed her.

"Here is a bowl of milk for you, Miss Kitty," said the little girl, "and a ball of yarn to play with."

So Miss Kitty settled down in her new home with a purr.

Mr. Pup found a boy in the house next door. The boy had a bone and some meat for Pup, a bed for him to sleep in, and a handsome collar to wear.

"Bow wow," barked Pup. "This is the home for me."

That night each one said, as he went to sleep, "At last I've found the best home of all, the very best home for me."